MATH ADVENTURES

KALA AND THE KITES

A SHAPES ADVENTURE

by Elizabeth Everett

illustrated by Amy Zhing

Tools for Parents & Teachers

Grasshopper Books enhance imagination and introduce the earliest readers to fiction with fun storylines and illustrations. The easy-to-read text supports early reading experiences with repetitive sentence patterns and sight words.

Before Reading

- Discuss the cover illustration. What do readers see?
- Look at the picture glossary together. Discuss the words.

Read the Book

- Read the book to the child, or have him or her read independently.
- "Walk" through the book and look at the illustrations. Who is the main character? What is happening in the story?

After Reading

- Prompt the child to think more. Ask: Kala and her brother recognize shapes in kites. What shapes did you see in the story?

Grasshopper Books are published by Jump!
5357 Penn Avenue South
Minneapolis, MN 55419
www.jumplibrary.com

Library of Congress Cataloging-in-Publication Data

Names: Everett, Elizabeth, author. | Zhing, Amy, illustrator.
Title: Kala and the kites: a shapes adventure
by Elizabeth Everett; illustrated by Amy Zhing.
Description: Minneapolis, MN: Jump!, Inc., [2023]
Series: Math adventures
Includes index. | Audience: Ages 5–8
Identifiers: LCCN 2021970007 (print)
LCCN 2021970008 (ebook)
ISBN 9781636908670 (hardcover)
ISBN 9781636908687 (paperback)
ISBN 9781636908694 (ebook)
Subjects: LCSH: Shapes—Juvenile literature.
Classification: LCC QA445.5 .E843 2023 (print)
LCC QA445.5 (ebook) | DDC 516/.15—dc23/eng/20220126
LC record available at https://lccn.loc.gov/2021970007
LC ebook record available at https://lccn.loc.gov/2021970008

Editor: Jenna Gleisner
Direction and Layout: Molly Ballanger
Illustrator: Amy Zhing

Printed in the United States of America at
Corporate Graphics in North Mankato, Minnesota.

Table of Contents

Different Shapes

Kala is excited to go to the park.

She helps her mom make sandwiches.

"Let's cut them into triangles!" Kala says.

Her little brother, Anil, is excited, too.

They ride their bikes to the park.

"Come on, Anil," says Kala.
"Let's follow the rectangles."

rectangle

"Look at the kite!" Kala shouts.

"It has squares," says Anil.

"Yes, Anil. And the two squares together make a rectangle," says Kala.

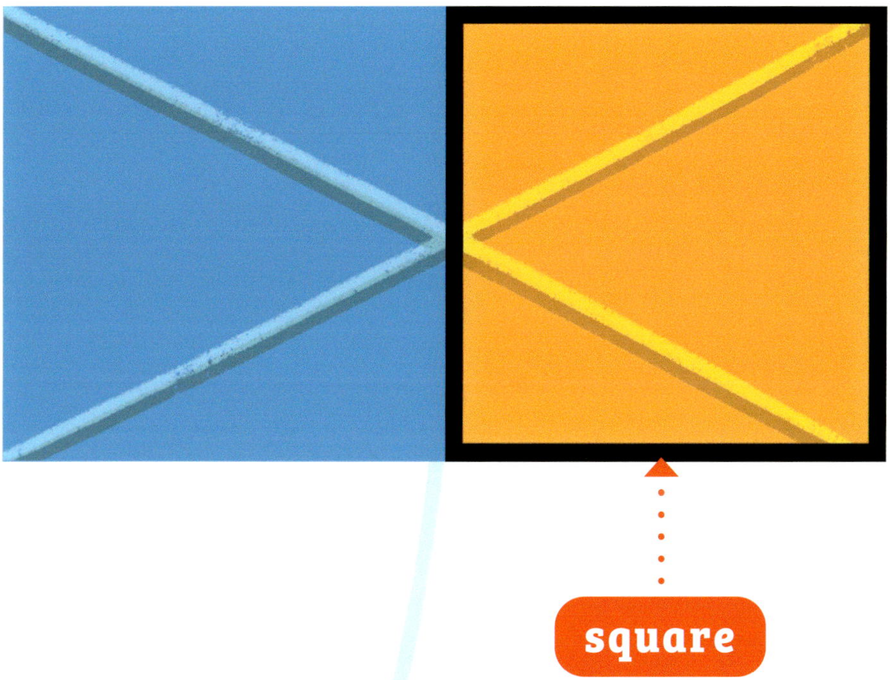

They keep riding.

“That’s a diamond!” says Anil.

“You’re right!” Kala says. “It’s a diamond made up of triangles.”

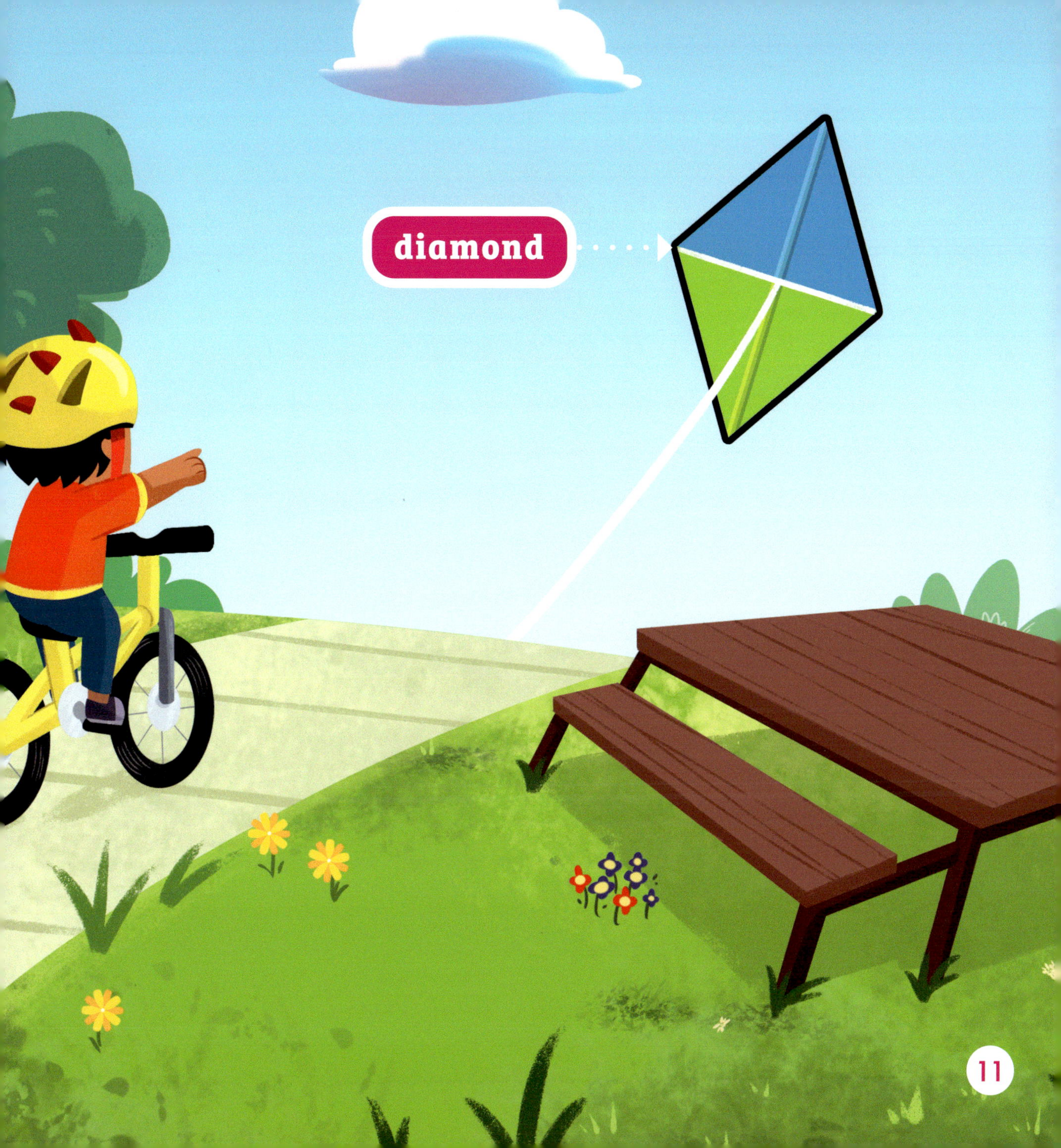
diamond

They stop to eat lunch.

Kala gives Anil half
of the sandwich.

"I'll eat this triangle,"
says Anil.

Kala smiles. "And I'll
eat this one!" she says.

The sky is full of shapes.

"More triangles!" says Anil.

"No, Anil. Triangles have three sides. That kite has four sides that are the same. It is a square," says Kala.

"But there are four triangles in the square," says Anil.

"Oh! Yes, I see them now!" says Kala.

"Anil, I have a surprise for you," says Kala. "Look at our kite!"

"Our kite is a circle," says Anil.

"Right. It is round and has no corners," Kala says.

"It's not flat anymore!" says Kala.
"Now it's a cylinder."

"Come on, Anil," says Kala.
"Let's fly it!"

Let's Review!

Kala and Anil point out shapes they see in kites. What shapes do you see in the kites below? Do any of them form other shapes?

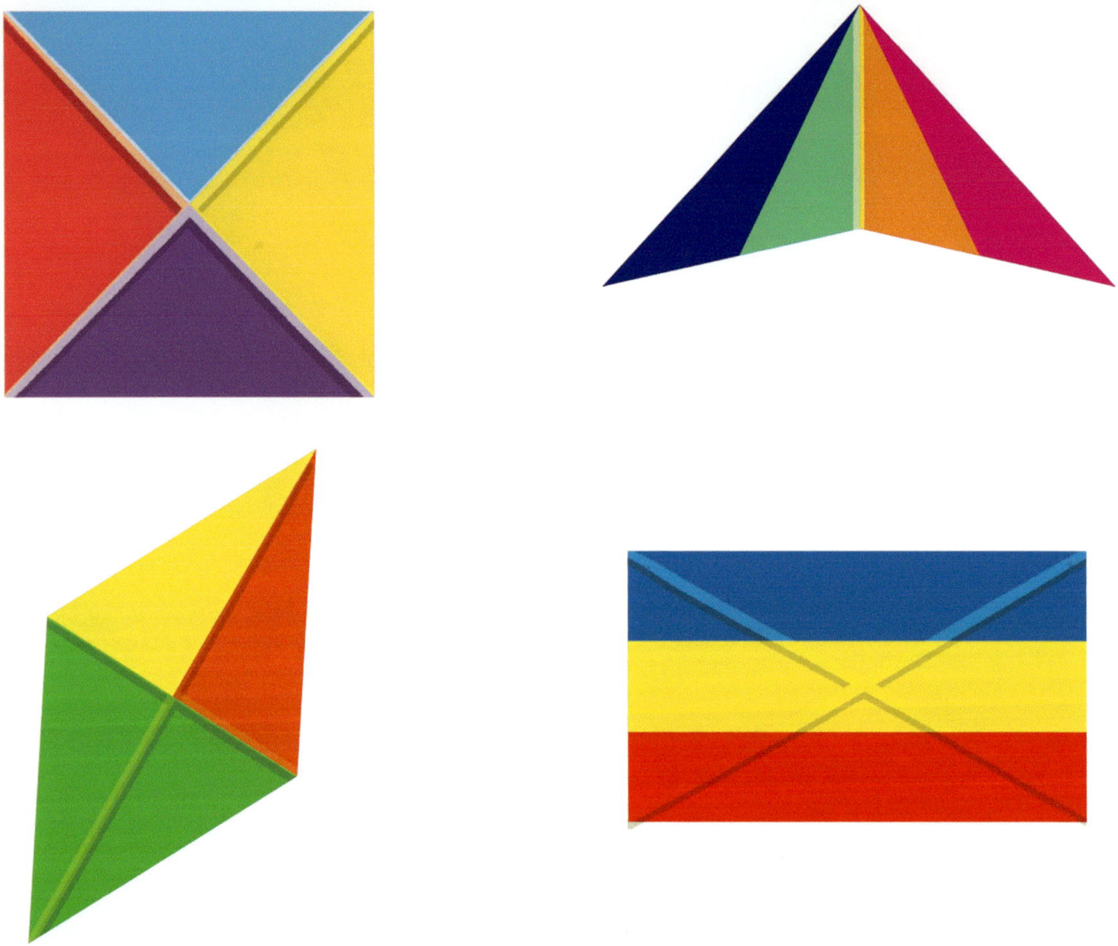

Picture Glossary

circle
A flat, perfectly round shape.

cylinder
A shape with flat, circular ends and sides shaped like the outside of a tube.

diamond
A flat shape with four equal sides, resting on one of its points.

rectangle
A flat shape with four sides and four right angles.

square
A flat shape with four straight, equal sides and four right angles.

triangle
A flat shape with three straight sides and three angles.

Index

To Learn More

Finding more information is as easy as 1, 2, 3.

1. Go to www.factsurfer.com
2. Enter "**Kalaandthekites**" into the search box.
3. Choose your book to see a list of websites.